Santa Claus

The Magical World of Father Christmas

CARLTON KiDS

The Land where Santa Claus Lives

One of the world's greatest unsolved mysteries can be found in the far north, at a place called the North Pole. The area around the North Pole, known as the Arctic, shivers under a sheet of ice and snow for much of the year. It includes the vast Arctic Ocean and parts of countries such as Russia, Canada, Finland, Norway, Sweden and Iceland. In winter, Arctic temperatures are colder than you could ever imagine (down to –68ºC (–90ºF)) and it stays dark all day. Even in summer, when the sun shines both day and night, the temperature is still freezing around the North Pole.

Laplanders from northern Scandinavia and the Inuit people of Alaska and Canada have always lived in the Arctic lands. But the most famous person to have made this his home is Santa Claus, or Father Christmas as he is also known. For centuries explorers and scientists have braved the bitter cold to discover all they can about the wonders of the Arctic. Aircraft have flown over the North Pole and submarines have sailed beneath it. We've learned a lot about this distant place, but one mystery still remains – where does Santa Claus live?

Life at the North Pole

If you stand at the North Pole it's a curious fact that, whichever way you turn, you will be facing south! The ice here is about four metres thick and is quite safe to stand on – unlike the thin layer of ice that forms on puddles and ponds at home in the winter.

North Pole

The Arctic

The word 'Arctic' comes from the Greek word meaning 'bear'. It refers to two constellations, or groups of stars, called the Great Bear and Little Bear that travel in the night sky around the North Pole. The real Arctic bear is, of course, the polar bear – often spotted by Arctic explorers. Occasionally, explorers also see small, strange creatures that they mistake for bears. These creatures hold the key to the North Pole's best-kept secret…

Santa's House

Santa's house is an old log cabin, built many centuries ago by Santa and the elves. You won't see it marked on any chart, and there are no signposts to guide the way but, once you step through the magic portal, you have only to follow the welcoming glow of lights and the lazy plume of smoke rising from the chimney to find it. Santa chose to live at the North Pole so he could go about his business without being disturbed. Yet, even in this far-away place, he had to protect his home with a curtain of magic, and the only way to reach it is through the enchanted portal.

The Igloo

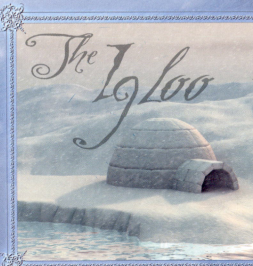

People who live in the Arctic, such as Eskimos, sometimes build temporary shelters out of snow. The most famous type of snow home is the igloo – a dome-shaped building made out of blocks of hard-packed snow. The blocks freeze together to form a strong, airtight structure that is cosy inside, needing only a single candle to keep it warm. Santa built his wonderful ice dome in the same way, using blocks of ice instead of snow.

Santa's house may look rather small from the outside but, in this enchanted land, things are not always as they seem. When you walk through the front door you are welcomed not by a tiny cottage living room, as you might expect, but by an enormous great hall with beautifully carved wooden walls and a dazzling fireplace at one end. Here, Santa and Mrs Claus spend their evenings, planning how to make each Christmas better than the last one. Here, too, Santa hosts fabulous parties for the elves.

The Elves at Work and Play

Making Christmas happen every year involves a lot of work, but Santa has the most trustworthy team of helpers you could ever wish for – a whole village of elves. Like their relatives the pixies, fairies and leprechauns, these enchanted creatures live in our world but avoid all human contact. Elves don't have such powerful magic as fairies but they are hard working. It was their skills as craftsmen, foresters and gardeners that made Santa choose them as his helpers.

The Grand Elf

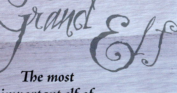

The most important elf of all is the Grand Elf – mayor of the elf village. The Grand Elf works closely with Santa and Mrs Claus to make sure the elves are happy in their work and that everything is running smoothly. Unlike the other elves, who may travel south to the great forests, the Grand Elf remains at the North Pole until he retires and a new Grand Elf is chosen.

The elves' natural home is in the great northern forests that stretch across Europe, Russia, Canada and North America. As spring approaches each year, a number of elves leave the elf village to return to the forests, making the long journey south across the ice before it starts to melt. Once back in their beloved homelands, they spend the summer chopping down trees to provide wood for fuel and for making toys. They also plant new trees to replace the ones they've cut down. When the ocean re-freezes, they make their way back north again, dragging sleds loaded with wood behind them.

The elves consider it a great honour to work for Santa. Many of them spend years living in the village, raising children who may one day work for Santa themselves. When ageing elves retire and head south, some of the older children accompany them to learn traditional elf skills. Only then will they decide whether to return to the North Pole. With a natural love of woodlands, not every elf is suited to life in the cold, white wilderness of the Arctic.

Some elves are specially trained to work with the reindeer. They raise the young animals in the village, caring for them and getting them used to wearing a harness. As the reindeer grow up, the elves help Santa decide which ones are best suited to working in the sleigh team.

The Christmas Tree

Christmas trees date back over 500 years, when people in Europe started bringing trees into their homes and hanging treats from the branches. Such treats included apples, dates, nuts, paper flowers and even cheese! Spruce, fir or pine trees were popular, because these stayed green longest after being cut down. Artificial trees first appeared in the 19th century and were made from goose feathers!

The Mail Room

When the toys are finished, they travel from the workshop to the mail room. Here they are wrapped, ready to be loaded onto Santa's sleigh. The mail room is also where Santa receives millions of letters from children all over the world. Santa reads every letter and can tell, just by looking at a child's name, whether the sender has been good or bad. He keeps a 'Naughty or Nice' list for each child. Santa knows all children are naughty sometimes and that, occasionally, that's how a child learns right from wrong. But, when a child does something very naughty, it makes him terribly sad. When all the Naughty or Nice lists are complete, Santa checks them twice and decides what each child deserves to get as a Christmas present.

UGANDA

UKRAINE

UNITED KINGDOM

URUGUAY

The elves working in the mail room collect all the letters that arrive from all over the world and carefully sort them. They arrange the letters by country, town and street so that, once Santa has read them all and decided who is to get what, the presents can be loaded onto the sleigh in the right order for delivery.

The mail room elves are very mischievous. They are always playing silly pranks on one another – putting glue on a stool just before someone sits down on it or using a little magic to make an envelope feel as heavy as an elephant. Mrs Claus keeps a watchful eye on the mail room elves. But none of the elves wants to let her down, so they never let their pranks get in the way of the job – at least, not for very long!

LOADING BAY

USA

WRAPPING BAY   READING ROOM

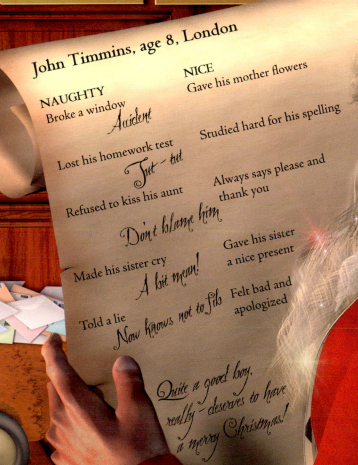

John Timmins, age 8, London

NAUGHTY
Broke a window
Accident

Lost his homework test
Tut – tut

Refused to kiss his aunt
Don't blame him

Made his sister cry
A bit mean!

Told a lie
Now knows not to fib

NICE
Gave his mother flowers

Studied hard for his spelling

Always says please and thank you

Gave his sister a nice present

Felt bad and apologized

Quite a good boy, really – deserves to have a merry Christmas!

Santa's Workshop

Santa's workshop is the noisiest place at the North Pole. Apart from when Santa holds a party (and that is quite often), the elves are at work all year round, making millions and millions of amazing toys. They work extremely hard, but they have lots of fun while they work. Santa encourages this because he knows that you only have as much fun playing with a toy as the elves put into making it!

The Teddy Bear

One of the world's most popular toys, the teddy bear, has been around since 1902. It gets its name from the American President Theodore Roosevelt, who was known as Teddy. The president had refused to shoot a bear cub while out hunting one day and, before long, toy-makers were selling 'teddy' bears to an eager public. Today, early toy bears made by the German toy company Steiff can fetch over £100,000! Of all the toys they make, teddy bears are the elves' favourite.

Elves learn very fast.
They can read, write and do the trickiest sums before they are three years old.
Then they learn useful skills such as wood carving and toy-making. Some even study electronics so that, one day, they'll be able to make complicated toys such as computer games and robots.

Inside the Workshop

Inside the workshop, there is a special room where a group of elves does nothing but invent new toys all day long. Santa is always on hand to help the elves in their work or to try out a new design. Mrs Claus, too, loves to help out in the workshop whenever she gets the chance.

When they are old enough, the young elves join the workshop where they spend their time helping the toy-makers and learning everything there is to know about making toys. In the evenings they study things like paint mixing, plastic moulding, bear stuffing and trumpet bending.

The workshop itself has hundreds of storeys that, in the real world, would run many miles underground. But, in this magical realm, there are windows on every floor, each looking out over a shimmering landscape of crisp white snow.

Mrs Claus

If there was a prize for the person who works hardest at the North Pole, everyone agrees it would go to Mrs Claus. One of her tasks is to oversee work in the kitchen, where the Christmas treats are made and meals are prepared for the elves and the reindeer. Mrs Claus has such a talent for organizing that she also plans all the work that goes on in the workshop, the mail room and the vegetable garden. Santa is the first to admit that Christmas is a very complicated affair. Without Mrs Claus's guiding hand, the whole operation would probably grind to a halt!

The Happy Couple

Santa Claus has always had the elves to help him, but his one regret was that he did not have someone special to share his happy home. Then, while travelling around the world one Christmas Eve, he met and fell in love with a woman whose spirit was so pure, and whose belief in him was so complete, that she was able to cross over into his magic realm. Their wedding was the most spectacular event ever seen, with all the kings and queens of the elves and fairies in attendance. Santa Claus and Mrs Claus are the happiest couple in the world because they spend their lives making sure everyone has a happy Christmas.

Thankfully, she's always there with a gentle reminder, telling Santa and the elves exactly what they need to do next. Despite her heavy workload, no one can ever remember seeing Mrs Claus without a smile on her face.

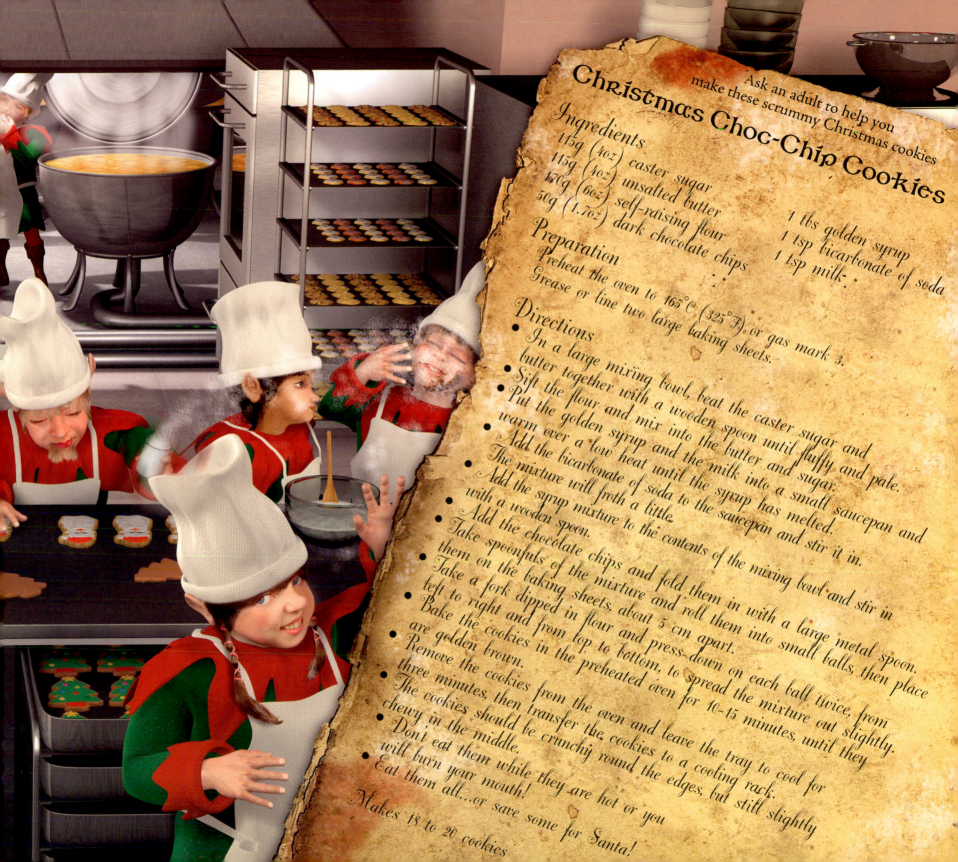

Christmas Choc-Chip Cookies

Ingredients

115g (4oz) caster sugar
115g (4oz) unsalted butter
170g (6oz) self-raising flour
50g (1.7oz) dark chocolate chips

1 tbs golden syrup
1 tsp bicarbonate of soda
1 tsp milk

Preparation

Preheat the oven to 165°C (325°F) or gas mark 3.
Grease or line two large baking sheets.

Directions

- In a large mixing bowl, beat the caster sugar and butter together with a wooden spoon until fluffy and pale.
- Sift the flour and mix into the butter and sugar.
- Put the golden syrup and the milk into a small saucepan and warm over a low heat until the syrup has melted.
- Add the bicarbonate of soda to the saucepan and stir it in. The mixture will froth a little.
- Add the syrup mixture to the contents of the mixing bowl and stir in with a wooden spoon.
- Add the chocolate chips and fold them in with a large metal spoon.
- Take spoonfuls of the mixture and roll them into small balls, then place them on the baking sheets, about 5 cm apart.
- Take a fork dipped in flour and press down on each ball twice, from left to right and from top to bottom, to spread the mixture out slightly.
- Bake the cookies in the preheated oven for 10-15 minutes, until they are golden brown.
- Remove the cookies from the oven and leave the tray to cool for three minutes, then transfer the cookies to a cooling rack.
- The cookies should be crunchy round the edges, but still slightly chewy in the middle.
- Don't eat them while they are hot or you will burn your mouth!
- Eat them all...or save some for Santa!

Makes 18 to 20 cookies

The Reindeer

RUDOLPH

Smaller than the other reindeer, but makes up for it by having more heart and more stamina than the rest, plus a very special nose...

The reindeer in the sleigh team fly with Santa every Christmas until they retire and return to the wild. Then they pass on their names – Cupid, Comet, Vixen – to newcomers who take their place. Training under the Sleigh Master, the new team members are taught how to dodge round buildings and sidestep trees in mid-air. They train for landing on rooftops by leaping on to steeply sloping sheets of ice, and practise over and over again that all-important leap into the air for take off. Only by trying their hardest, and believing they can do it, can reindeer fly – belief is the key to the magic of flight.

Of all the reindeer, only Rudolph never retires. One winter, a long, long time ago, the fairies watched from their workroom as Rudolph started his training. They could see he was using every ounce of effort and that he wanted to fly with the team more than anything else. He was small, but he had an unbeatable spirit. That's why, when a thick fog descended that Christmas Eve, the fairies gave Rudolph his red nose.

DANCER

Legs are strong and muscular, and slightly longer than those of other team members. The most graceful reindeer in the team, although not the largest.

VIXEN

Very clever and strong-willed. Can be relied upon never to give up, even in the worst weather. Usually harnessed alongside Dancer.

PRANCER

Full of fun and energy. If ever the sleigh team is flagging, it needs only to look to Prancer to put a spring back in its step.

DASHER

Always ready and willing, with lots of energy to spare. Usually harnessed alongside Prancer, helping to fill the team with enthusiasm for the journey.

Antlers

Both male and female reindeer have large, branched horns called antlers. Each year, they shed their old antlers and start to grow new ones. To begin with, the new antlers are covered in a soft fur called velvet, but this soon drops off once the antlers become hard enough. The antlers then continue to grow, developing their distinctive shape.

The fog might have spread doubt among the team, ruining their belief that they could fly. But with Rudolph leading the way, his red nose glowing brightly, the other reindeer could see the magic working and had the confidence to fly around the world. Rudolph was such an inspiration to the sleigh team that, like Santa, he became part of the magic of Christmas, and is the only reindeer who is never replaced.

DONNER

he most powerful of the reindeer. His hoof-beats sound like the rumble of distant thunder – in fact, 'donner' means 'thunder' in German. He's always harnessed alongside Blitzen.

BLITZEN

The fastest reindeer in the sleigh team, Blitzen is named after the German word for 'lightning'. Even before he began training with the Sleigh Master, he could reach over 100 km/h.

COMET

Not as fast as Blitzen, but fast enough to give the 'lightning' reindeer a run for his money. Can be relied on to stay on course, no matter how strongly the winds blow.

CUPID

Flies straight as an arrow, with a keen sense of direction that always keeps him on course. Usually harnessed alongside Comet.

Santa's Magic Snowsuit

Everyone knows that Santa wears a bright red suit, but did you know he used to wear green? Many years ago, Santa would set out on Christmas Eve wearing a beautiful green woollen coat and trousers made for him by the elf tailors. Green is a favourite colour of the elves because it reminds them of their leafy woodland home. The woollen suit was thickly woven, heavy and warm, but, after many years of protecting Santa against the worst of the winter weather, it became rather worn.

The elf tailors knew that Santa needed a new suit and were determined to make him the most wonderful outfit ever worn. They asked the fairies to help them find the best cloth, and the fairies travelled the world gathering the finest spiders' silk. Then they spun the silk into yarn, using fairy spinning wheels, and wove the yarn into cloth on wooden looms. And when they showed the cloth to Santa Claus, he was amazed.

'This is the most marvellous cloth I have ever seen,' he said. 'It's as light as air and shimmers like the mist. I can see only one thing wrong with it. If I wear a suit made from this, I will shimmer too – like a misty ghost! I don't want to frighten young children who spot me on Christmas Eve!'

The fairies all giggled. They had already thought of this. Their final touch was to make the material as cosy as possible, so they conjured a magical spell that captured the soft dry warmth of a summer sunset and bathed the cloth in a rosy crimson glow. By the time the elf tailors had finished Santa's suit, the different layers of the magical fabric had combined to give the rich red colour that is now so familiar to us all.

Spiders' Silk Cloth

Spiders' silk is one of the strongest materials in the world, stronger even than steel. Yet the strands are soft and can stretch up to half their length without breaking. This enabled the fairies to give their cloth magical properties. The fibres in each layer of Santa's suit can become fluffier or thinner according to the weather, helping to keep Santa warm in cold climates and cool in hot ones. The cloth is so tough that, when they made Santa's suit, the tailor elves couldn't cut it with normal scissors. So the fairies cut it for them by flitting along each marked seam and dissolving the threads with their wands.

Fur Trim

The soft fur trim on the collar and cuffs of Santa's suit, as well as his hood, is there to protect his neck and wrists should ice ever form on his suit. Each spring apprentice elf tailors gather white fur shed by creatures such as the Arctic hare and use it to weave fresh fur trim for Santa's suit.

The Sleigh

Santa's Sleigh Specifications

Length	4 metres (13 feet)
Full length with reindeer harnessed	15 metres (49 feet)
Height	2 metres (6.5 feet)
Power	9 reindeer (4 pairs, one lead)
Top speed	50 km/h (30 mph)

SPECIAL EQUIPMENT

Altitude regulator
Water cooler
Enchanted cargo hold
Jingle bells

Food warmer
Positioning globe
Lightning lamps
Fairy dust store

Bubble-timer
Silencer skids
Eye-shade
Cookie jar

During its hectic voyage around the world on Christmas Eve, Santa's sleigh is battered by snowstorms one minute, and baked in the scorching heat of the sun the next.

When the sleigh returns to the North Pole, the elves whose job it is to look after it know that, once the Christmas party is over, they will have a tough time repairing the sleigh and restoring it to tip-top condition.

Santa's sleigh has many special features. These include jingle bells – like those on the reindeer's harnesses – that Santa silences simply by whispering 'Shh!'; a food warmer to keep the reindeer's moss and lichen pies hot; and a water cooler to provide cold drinks while visiting hot countries. It's important that the reindeer are properly fed and watered so they have the energy to work their magic and fly round the world.

LIGHTNING LAMPS – *each one contains a bolt of summer lightning. Santa simply removes the blackout disc from the lens to light up the night sky.*

ENCHANTED CARGO HOLD – *magic compartment where the presents are kept. It never gets full, no matter how much is stored there.*

STEALTH SHOCK ABSORBERS – *allow Santa to make quiet and gentle rooftop landings.*

SILENCER SKIDS – *special runners that carry the sleigh across the snow with barely a whisper.*

Normally, a reindeer can run at almost 80 km/h but, when pulling a loaded sleigh, Santa's team can only manage about 50 km/h. At that speed it would take a whole month to travel round the world! Luckily, thanks to a sprinkling of fairy dust and Santa's magic 'bubble-timer', when the reindeer take to the skies time just disappears.

ALTITUDE REGULATOR – *controls the height at which the sleigh is flying.*

BUBBLE-TIMER – *stops time so Santa and his team can travel the world in a single night.*

POSITIONING GLOBE – *tells Santa where he is in the world.*

Special Features

The two most interesting gadgets on Santa's sleigh are the positioning globe and the bubble-timer. Both rely on powerful magic. The globe is an exact model of the Earth that hovers, suspended in a beam of pure light, just in front of Santa's seat. A pulse of red light on the globe shows Santa exactly where he is in the world. A similar, larger version of the positioning globe sits in the great hall at the North Pole, so that everyone can keep track of Santa's progress.

The bubble-timer uses the most powerful magic of all. It is a glass ball filled with thick gel. When the ball is spun, lots of bubbles appear and join together to make one big bubble. The sleigh is then suspended in its own time 'bubble' that makes time stand still, enabling Santa to make his journey round the world in just one night. As the bubble inside the timer slowly dissolves back into smaller bubbles, the magic wears off and the ball must be spun again.

On Christmas Eve, Santa sets out from his home in the North Pole to begin his long journey around the world. First, he travels south across the Arctic Ocean and down into the Pacific, where he visits countries such as Australia and New Zealand. His work begins here because this is where the sun first rises on each new day, and where people first celebrate on Christmas morning.

a whole day to fly in a straight line around the Earth. But Santa, with all his zig-zagging back and forth, travels millions of times further than this. And he has to do it all in a single night! He simply couldn't manage it without his magic bubble-timer, which makes time stand still as he races from one place to another.

Travelling the World

From here, Santa follows a zig-zag route, from north to south and back again, rapidly moving westwards across the globe and always staying ahead of the dawn. Because time is different in different parts of the world, when Santa is in Paris, children in New Zealand will have opened their presents and be getting ready for lunch. And, as he delivers gifts in New York, it will be breakfast time in London.

Santa could never cover such vast distances without a little magical help. Even travelling very fast, it would normally take

Reindeer prefer the cold so, when visiting warm countries such as India and Brazil, Santa flies high in the sky where the air is cool. To stay on course, he uses gigantic landmarks like the Himalayan Mountains or the mighty Amazon River to guide him. In colder countries, Santa flies lower, using tall buildings such as the Eiffel Tower or the Empire State Building to guide him. Sometimes, when there's low cloud or heavy snow, he has to fly lower still to see where he's going, and that's when he's most often spotted.

Snow

The snow you use to make a snowman is actually a collection of crystal flakes that form when water high up in the clouds freezes. This then falls as snow. Snowflakes can clump together as they drift earthwards, but begin their journey quite separately. Snowflake crystals usually grow six very similar 'arms', like a star, as they freeze. Each flake freezes in its own little space in the cloud, so the chance of ever finding two snowflakes that are exactly the same is very unlikely. Each snowflake is almost as unique as a person's fingerprint.

Delivering the Presents

Santa Claus is famous for coming down the chimney, but don't worry if your home doesn't have one. He can transform himself into a shower of fairy dust and waft in under a door or even through a keyhole if necessary. After all, Santa is quite stout so even sliding down the chimney requires a little bit of magic and a lot of fairy dust!

Santa has a way with animals, so dogs won't bark at him and cats won't hiss. He's also an expert on Christmas customs. He knows that in some countries children hang stockings up for him to stuff with gifts, while in others they put shoes out instead. One of the traditions Santa likes best is when people leave cookies and a glass of milk out for him. Any cookies he doesn't eat himself he puts in a special jar on his sleigh and takes home for the elves' Christmas party. The reindeer like it too when apples and carrots are left out for them.

Santa prefers to visit children while they are sound asleep. That way, he doesn't have to stop for a chat or to tell a story, which would slow him down too much. You can't fool Santa — he knows when you're sleeping and when you're awake. If you do ever see him, it's because he's decided that you should.

Traces of Santa Claus

No matter how early you wake on Christmas morning you can be sure of one thing – Santa Claus will have been and gone. And, because you're so excited about opening your presents, you'll probably forget to look for traces he may have left behind – a light sprinkling of fairy dust on the curtains or a boot print on the carpet. By the time you've torn the wrapping paper from your gifts, all the evidence will have been lost forever.

Sightings of Santa

Some people would have you believe that no one's ever seen Santa Claus. Nothing could be further from the truth. Santa has been seen countless times over the years – how else would we know what he looks like? He has been spotted, of course, on Christmas Eve, but also at times when those seeing him – or even speaking to him – might not have realized who he was.

Santa doesn't just travel the world at Christmas. He likes to take trips at other times of the year as well, watching people and listening to them talk, learning about new trends. He never wears his red suit on these trips, but there is no disguising his long white beard or the twinkle in his eye. Watch out for him walking down your street!

Santa Claus in Outer Space

On 21 December, 1968, three NASA astronauts in an Apollo spacecraft made history when they blasted off from the Earth's surface to become the first men to orbit, or fly around, the Moon. They spent 20 hours circling the Moon, and each time they passed behind it they lost radio contact with Earth, so no one knew if they were still OK. When the spacecraft appeared from behind the Moon for the last time on Christmas Day, the astronaut James Lovell announced, 'Please be informed that there is a Santa Claus.' To this day, no one can be sure if he was joking or if he really did spot Santa on the far side of the Moon.

You can also see Santa in his grotto at Christmastime. He has many helpers who stand in for him in department stores around the world, but he also likes to put in an appearance as often as he can. So next time you visit Santa's grotto, you won't know whether you're talking to the real Santa or one of his helpers.

Christmas Day at the North Pole

A s Santa zig-zags across the world delivering presents on Christmas Eve, the elves begin to gather in the great hall. There are still lots of things to do after they've waved Santa goodbye on his journey – the stables must be prepared for the return of the sleigh team, the vegetable gardens must be tended, the workshop must be cleaned, the mail room must be cleared. But as the minutes tick by on Christmas Eve, the elves are eager to follow Santa's progress on the positioning globe in the great hall. They've spent all year working towards this moment and, as tension mounts, barely a word is spoken – a remarkable feat for the chatterbox elves.

As dawn breaks, the elves watch the glowing dot of red light on the globe approach the North Pole, heralding Santa's return. Then, when they hear the sound of the sleigh bells outside, the room erupts with cheers and laughter, and everyone rushes outside to welcome Santa home.